The Case of Missing Sandwich

Mrigendra Bharti

Published by Sellbrochure Vymish Entertainment, 2024.

This is a work of fiction. Similarities to real people, places, or events are entirely coincidental.

THE CASE OF MISSING SANDWICH

First edition. July 15, 2024.

Copyright © 2024 Mrigendra Bharti.

ISBN: 979-8227191151

Written by Mrigendra Bharti.

Table of Contents

Preface

In the sterile heart of Acme Enterprises, where the hum of fluorescent lights battled the drone of office chatter, a most peculiar crime unfolded. It wasn't a case of embezzlement or stolen staplers, but a much more personal violation – the lunchtime heist of a perfectly good sandwich.

Sarah, a champion of healthy lunches and meticulous meal planning, found herself staring at the empty betrayal between two slices of bread.

This wasn't just hunger pangs, it was a culinary caper! Join us as we delve into the mystery of the missing sandwich. Was it a desperate colleague, a mischievous office prankster, or perhaps a rogue office gremlin with a penchant for protein?

Prepare for a tale of lunchtime intrigue, where accusations fly faster than cafeteria trays, and the only weapon is a well-honed sense of humor (and maybe a spare protein bar). So, grab your metaphorical magnifying glass and pack your sense of adventure, because we're about to embark on a delicious whodunit – The Case of the Missing Sandwich.

Prologue

The fluorescent lights of the Acme Enterprises break room cast a harsh glare on the meticulously organized shelves of snacks and the overflowing fridge. It was a haven of predictability, a lunchtime oasis in a sea of cubicles and deadlines. Or so Sarah thought.

As she reached for her lunch bag, a familiar weight promised a comforting midday ritual – a carefully constructed sandwich, the culmination of a week's worth of healthy lunch planning. But a single, horrifying glance inside shattered that illusion. The space between the bread slices gaped accusingly, devoid of the vibrant colors of roasted turkey and crisp lettuce. Her perfectly planned lunch had vanished.

Panic gnawed at the edges of Sarah's stomach, a feeling far more potent than mere hunger. Had she forgotten to pack it? Impossible. Had some rogue creature pilfered her precious creation? The answer, however absurd it seemed at first, would lead Sarah on a delightful, bite-sized adventure, one that would unravel the mystery of the missing sandwich and reveal a hidden truth about her colleagues – a truth far tastier than she could have ever imagined.

About Sellbrochure Vymish Entertainment

Sellbrochure Vymish Entertainment, recognized as India's largest book publishing company, has made significant strides in ensuring its extensive collection of books reaches audiences across the global market. This rapid expansion is a testament to the company's dedication to disseminating knowledge and literature far beyond national borders. Central to its success is its affiliation with InkWhirl Media Networks, a reputable entity in the media and publication industry known for its innovative and strategic approaches. Within this network, InkWhirl Publication LLC operates as a vital division, further enhancing the company's capabilities and reach in the international market.

The visionary behind this enterprise is Mrigendra Bharti, the founder of Sellbrochure Vymish Entertainment. His foresight and passion for the literary world have been instrumental in steering the company towards remarkable growth and recognition. Under his leadership, Sellbrochure Vymish Entertainment has not only expanded its catalog but also established a strong presence in both domestic and international markets. Mrigendra Bharti's commitment to excellence and innovation has been a driving force in the company's journey, ensuring that it stays ahead of industry trends and meets the evolving needs of readers worldwide.

Sellbrochure Vymish Entertainment operates under the robust support of its parental organization, Mrigendra Bharti Group InfoTech. This affiliation provides the necessary resources and strategic guidance, enabling the publishing company to undertake ambitious projects and explore new markets. Mrigendra Bharti Group InfoTech's extensive experience in technology and information services has been a valuable asset, allowing Sellbrochure Vymish Entertainment to integrate advanced digital solutions in its operations, thereby enhancing its distribution capabilities and reader engagement.

Through relentless efforts and a commitment to quality, Sellbrochure Vymish Entertainment continues to break barriers and expand the reach of Indian literature globally. The company's diverse portfolio includes a wide range of genres, catering to different age groups and interests, thereby fostering a rich and inclusive reading culture. As it continues to innovate and grow, Sellbrochure Vymish Entertainment remains dedicated to its mission of making literature accessible to all, contributing significantly to the global literary landscape.

Connect With Mrigendra,
Thank you very much for choosing this book.
You can also connect with me on Instagram,
https://www.instagram.com/i_mrigendrabharti.official
With Love,
Mrigendra Bharti

Introduction

In the fluorescent-lit labyrinth of Acme Enterprises, the midday break was a sacred ritual. Phones were silenced, keyboards lay dormant, and the air hummed with the satisfying clinking of Tupperware containers being unsealed. For Sarah, a champion of healthy lunches and meticulous meal planning, lunchtime was a moment of peace amidst the corporate chaos. Today, however, that peace was shattered.

Reaching for her lunch bag, the familiar weight promised a delicious culmination of her efforts – a vibrant masterpiece of roasted turkey, crisp lettuce, and tangy cranberry sauce nestled between two slices of whole-wheat bread. But as she peered inside, a gasp escaped her lips. The space between the bread slices lay empty, a mocking expanse of disappointment staring back at her. Her meticulously crafted sandwich, the cornerstone of her carefully planned lunch, had vanished.

Panic, a feeling far sharper than mere hunger, clawed at Sarah. A stolen lunch? In this sterile, corporate haven? Had she forgotten to pack it? Impossible, the weight of the bag in her hand confirmed its presence. Had some mythical office gremlin, a creature of legend whispered about by sleep-deprived interns, developed a taste for gourmet turkey? The answer, however ridiculous it might seem at first, would propel Sarah on a delightful, bite-sized adventure. It was a quest that would not only solve the mystery of the missing sandwich but also unveil a hidden truth about her colleagues – a truth far more delicious than she could have ever imagined.

Chapter 1: The Sandwich Disappears

Part 1: A Culinary Masterpiece

The fluorescent lights of the Acme Enterprises break room cast a sterile glow on Sarah's desk as she meticulously assembled her lunch. Tuesdays were for tuna salad, and this Tuesday, Sarah was determined to craft a culinary masterpiece. Her tuna salad wasn't your average mayo-and-canned-fish concoction. It was a symphony of flavors and textures, a testament to Sarah's dedication to the midday meal.

First came the bread, two slices of whole-wheat goodness toasted to a perfect golden brown. Onto one slice, Sarah spread a generous layer of creamy avocado, its subtle nuttiness a perfect base for what was to come. Next, she flaked a can of high-quality tuna in olive oil, discarding any rogue flakes that dared to appear dry or underseasoned.

But the true magic began with the extras. A sprinkle of chopped red onion added a welcome piquant bite, balanced by the sweetness of diced dried cranberries. Sliced celery provided a refreshing crunch, while crumbled feta cheese offered a salty tang. A drizzle of balsamic glaze tied everything together, its sweet and tangy notes creating a flavor explosion on the palate.

As Sarah meticulously arranged these ingredients into a work of edible art, a sense of accomplishment washed over her. This wasn't just lunch; it was a reward for a long morning spent battling spreadsheets and budget reports. It was a moment of pure, unadulterated joy, a tiny oasis in the often-mundane world of corporate accounting.

Carefully wrapping the sandwich in its designated lunch bag, a vibrantly colored whale frolicking amidst cartoon waves, Sarah secured it with a matching whale-shaped clip. A small smile played on her lips as she placed it in the communal refrigerator, nestled amongst the usual Tupperware containers and yogurt cups. It was a place of honor, reserved for her culinary creations, and today's masterpiece deserved nothing less.

Little did Sarah know, her carefully crafted tuna salad sandwich was about to embark on an unexpected journey, one that would transform a simple lunch into a legendary office caper.

Part 2: A Vanished Lunch

The afternoon sun cast long shadows across Sarah's desk as she tackled a mountain of invoices. The satisfying crunch of a carrot stick provided a brief respite from the monotony, but her mind kept drifting back to her lunch. Hunger gnawed at her stomach, and she envisioned each delightful bite of her tuna masterpiece.

With a relieved sigh, she pushed back from her desk and headed towards the refrigerator, her stomach grumbling in anticipation. Reaching for the handle, a wave of unease washed over her. The familiar weight of her lunch bag was absent. Panic clawed at her throat as she peered inside the fridge. The shelf that usually held her vibrantly colored whale lunch bag was bare.

Her heart hammered against her ribs. Had she imagined packing it? Impossible. The memory of meticulously crafting the sandwich and securing it with the whale clip was vivid. Maybe someone had borrowed it by mistake? But who would take her lunch, especially a lunch adorned with such a conspicuous bag?

Confusion morphed into anger. Stealing someone's lunch was a cardinal sin in any office, a violation of the unwritten social contract of shared break rooms and communal refrigerators. Sarah scanned the faces of her colleagues, hoping to catch a glimpse of someone suspiciously munching on a tuna-laden sandwich. But everyone seemed engrossed in their work, oblivious to the growing turmoil within her.

Taking a deep breath, Sarah decided to approach the situation logically. Perhaps there was a reasonable explanation. Maybe the cleaning crew had accidentally misplaced her lunch bag. Or maybe there was a new office policy about labeling food that she wasn't aware of. With a sliver of hope clinging to these possibilities, Sarah set off on a mission to solve the mystery of the missing masterpiece.

Part 3: A Call to Action

Sarah's first stop was Brenda, the ever-smiling office manager who knew everything that went on within the walls of Acme Enterprises. Brenda, perched behind her mountain of files, listened patiently to Sarah's frantic explanation. A frown creased her brow as she shook her head.

"No new lunch policies, Sarah. And the cleaning crew doesn't touch personal belongings. They just empty the trash and wipe down the surfaces."

Disappointment gnawed at Sarah. If Brenda didn't have any answers, then who did? As Sarah recounted her tale of the missing sandwich to Brenda, a voice piped up from the cubicle next door.

It was Tom, the tech-savvy member of the accounting department and Sarah's closest work confidante. Tom, with his mop of unruly hair and perpetually tired eyes, was a wizard with computers and a fountain of quirky ideas.

"Sounds like a job for the A-Team," Tom declared, a mischievous glint in his eyes.

Sarah, initially confused, raised an eyebrow. "The A-Team? What are you talking about?"

Tom rolled back in his chair, a grin spreading across his face. "The Acme Enterprises Detective Agency, of course! You, the victim of the culinary crime, and me, the brilliant tech investigator. We'll need a third member, though.

Someone with a nose for sniffing out clues, someone like..."

His gaze darted towards Nancy's cubicle, where the perpetually curious intern was meticulously organizing a filing cabinet. Nancy, with her fiery red hair and insatiable thirst for knowledge, was the perfect fit for the role of investigator extraordinaire.

Tom's plan was audacious, bordering on ridiculous. But as Sarah stared at the empty space on the fridge shelf, a flicker of determination ignited within her. Retrieving her stolen lunch wasn't just about satisfying her hunger; it was about the principle of the thing. Someone had violated the sanctity of her lunch, and that crime wouldn't go unpunished.

Taking a deep breath, Sarah straightened her shoulders. "Alright, Tom. Let's do this."

Part 4: The Investigation Begins

With Tom as the tech whiz and Nancy as the ace investigator, Sarah, the lunchtime victim, formed an unlikely detective trio. Their first order of business: brainstorming. They huddled around Sarah's desk, the remnants of her morning bagel scattered like breadcrumbs (a not-so-subtle metaphor, Nancy quipped).

"We need a plan," Tom declared, tapping his fingers on the keyboard. "First, let's establish a timeline. When did you last see your lunch, Sarah?"

Sarah recounted the meticulous assembly process, placing the time around 10:30 am. She remembered taking a quick coffee break around 11:00 am, but her lunch bag was still there.

"Okay," Tom chimed in, "so it went missing sometime between 11:00 am and whenever you went for lunch."

Nancy, ever the detail-oriented one, piped up.

"Did anyone seem suspicious around that time? Anyone lingering by the fridge, acting shifty?"

Sarah shook her head. The break room had been a constant hum of activity throughout the morning, with people grabbing snacks and reheating leftovers. It would have been hard to pinpoint anyone acting out of the ordinary.

Tom, however, had a different approach. "The key might be in the lunch bag itself," he mused, his eyes lighting up. "We can track its movements electronically."

Confused, Sarah raised an eyebrow. "Electronically? My lunch bag is made of fabric, not microchips."

Tom chuckled. "Not the bag itself, Sarah. The whale clip. Remember, it's metal. Most modern buildings have security scanners at the entrance and exit. If someone with the clip left the building, it might have triggered a security ping."

A flicker of hope ignited in Sarah's eyes. Maybe Tom, with his tech wizardry, was onto something.

With renewed determination, the makeshift detective agency set out on their mission. Tom would liaise with security to check for any suspicious pings, while Nancy would interview potential witnesses in the break room. Sarah, the aggrieved party, would create a detailed description of the missing masterpiece, complete with a sketch of its vibrant whale exterior.

As they embarked on their investigation, one thing was certain: the mystery of the missing tuna sandwich had transformed a mundane Tuesday afternoon into an adventure. Who would have thought that a simple lunch could spark such intrigue? Little did they know, the case of the missing sandwich was just beginning, and its ripples would soon spread throughout the entire office.

Chapter 2: Following the Crumb Trail

Part 1: A Glimmer of Hope

The fluorescent lights of the Acme Enterprises break room seemed to buzz with anticipation as Nancy, Sarah, and Tom huddled around the fridge. Their initial investigation had yielded little in the way of concrete leads. Security had no record of the whale clip triggering any exit sensors, and interviews with colleagues proved fruitless. Disappointment hung heavy in the air, thick enough to spread on toast (though perhaps not Sarah's favorite avocado toast).

Just as Sarah was about to resign herself to a dinner of vending machine misery, Nancy, ever the optimist, let out a gasp.

"Wait a minute!" she exclaimed, her eyes gleaming with excitement. "There is something... a clue!"

She pointed towards a narrow gap between the refrigerator and the counter. Nestled precariously amongst the dust bunnies and forgotten yogurt cup lids was a tiny, glistening object – a single bread crumb. It wasn't much, but to Nancy's trained eye, it was a beacon of hope in the vast sea of lunchtime monotony.

"A bread crumb?" Sarah echoed, her voice devoid of enthusiasm. "That could be from anyone's lunch."

"Maybe," Nancy conceded, a sly grin spreading across her face. "But most people don't eat tuna salad sandwiches with sun-dried tomato focaccia bread."

Sarah's eyes widened. The bread crumb, upon closer inspection, did indeed have a distinct reddish hue, a telltale sign of her unusual bread choice. A spark of excitement ignited within her. Could this be the break they'd been waiting for?

Tom, ever the pragmatist, interjected. "One bread crumb isn't exactly a smoking gun, Nancy. But it is a start. We just need to follow the trail."

The break room floor, unfortunately, wasn't littered with a Hansel-and-Gretel-esque path of breadcrumbs leading to the missing sandwich.

But Sarah, with a newfound determination, crouched down and scrutinized the area around the refrigerator. Her keen eye spotted another glint amongst the debris – a second, slightly larger bread crumb.

Following this new lead, they traced a path across the linoleum floor, the bread crumbs acting as a cryptic map towards the truth. The trail led them past deserted desks and overflowing wastebaskets, the silence broken only by the rhythmic hum of the office machinery.

With each bread crumb they found, their hope grew. This wasn't just random crumbs; they were a deliberate trail, left behind by the culprit in their haste or perhaps as a taunting message. The question was, who would be so brazen as to leave such an incriminating trail?

Part 2: The Culprit Revealed

The trail of breadcrumbs led the unlikely detective trio on a meandering journey through the labyrinthine cubicles of Acme Enterprises.

Sarah, fueled by a growing sense of determination and a rumbling stomach, meticulously collected each crumb in a crumpled napkin, their evidence bag for this unconventional investigation.

Tom, his eyes glued to the ever-growing breadcrumb path on his phone screen (thanks to a handy breadcrumb-recognition app he'd downloaded), navigated their course. Nancy, ever the theorist, spun elaborate scenarios about the culprit's motives.

"Maybe it's a disgruntled intern," she whispered, her voice laced with dramatic flair, "seeking revenge for years of fetching coffee and filing endless reports!"

"Or perhaps," Tom chimed in, his brow furrowed in concentration, "it's a master thief with a specific craving for tuna salad on sun-dried tomato focaccia."

Sarah, torn between amusement and exasperation, rolled her eyes. "Let's keep it grounded, people. This is most likely someone who just wanted a quick lunch and panicked when they realized it wasn't theirs."

The trail of crumbs led them past the ever-chatting marketing team, oblivious to the culinary caper unfolding mere feet away. They weaved through the silent graveyard of empty cubicles, remnants of unfinished reports and cold coffee cups hinting at the usual workday hustle.

Finally, the breadcrumb trail reached a dead end – a deserted corner cubicle with a single, wilting philodendron plant as its only occupant.

Disappointment washed over Sarah. Had the trail gone cold? Had the culprit cleverly diverted their breadcrumb path to throw them off track?

Just as Sarah was about to voice her concerns, Nancy, ever the observant one, let out a triumphant cry. Tucked beneath the lip of the empty desk, partially obscured by a discarded newspaper, was a glint of vibrant color – the unmistakable blue of Sarah's whale-shaped lunch bag clip.

Hope surged through Sarah's veins. They had found the missing piece, or at least a piece, of the puzzle. But where was the lunch bag itself, and more importantly, the delicious sandwich it contained? With renewed determination, they scanned the cubicle, their eyes searching for any sign of the missing lunch.

Their search was rewarded when Tom, peering under the desk with the flashlight on his phone, spotted a telltale bulge in the bottom drawer. Reaching in cautiously, he pulled out a vibrantly colored whale lunch bag, slightly crumpled but otherwise intact. Relief washed over Sarah as she recognized her missing culinary masterpiece.

Part 3: A Grumpy Confession

The recovery of the lunch bag sent a wave of exhilaration through the makeshift detective agency. Sarah snatched the bag from Tom, a triumphant smile lighting up her face. Relief battled with a surge of anger – relief that her precious sandwich was safe, anger at the culprit who had dared to steal her lunch.

But before she could tear into the bag and reclaim her culinary masterpiece, Nancy placed a restraining hand on her arm.

"Hold on, Sarah," she said, her voice laced with caution. "We can't just assume the sandwich is safe. The culprit might have tampered with it in some way."

Sarah's smile faltered. The possibility hadn't occurred to her, but the thought of a sabotaged sandwich sent shivers down her spine. Tom, ever the pragmatist, chimed in with a solution.

"We need to examine the contents before you declare victory," he suggested, his eyes scanning the lunch bag for any signs of tampering.

With careful hands, Sarah unclipped the whale clip and peered inside. Relief washed over her again. The sandwich, nestled between two ice packs, appeared untouched. The avocado spread remained a vibrant green, the diced cranberries a jewel-toned red. It looked exactly as she had left it, a testament to her meticulous construction skills.

A wave of hunger pangs gnawed at her stomach. The ordeal had taken longer than expected, and the aroma of tuna salad wafting from the bag was nothing short of torture. But Sarah knew they weren't quite done yet. The mystery of the missing lunch remained unsolved. The culprit was still out there, and they craved justice (and perhaps a bite of that delicious sandwich).

"We need to find who did this," Sarah declared, her voice firm with resolve. "Someone had the audacity to steal my lunch, and they need to face the consequences."

Nancy, ever the strategist, suggested setting a trap. They could replace the sandwich with something less appealing, perhaps a decoy filled with questionable ingredients – think extra-pickled onions and week-old cottage cheese. The culprit, lured by the familiar lunch bag, would be caught red-handed (or rather, red-mouthed) upon taking a bite.

Tom, however, wasn't a fan of the revenge plot.

"Let's not stoop to their level," he argued. "We should confront the culprit, but in a civilized manner. Maybe they have a reasonable explanation."

Sarah weighed both options. A part of her craved revenge, a public display of the culprit's lunchtime transgression. But another part, the more logical one, agreed with Tom. Perhaps there was a genuine reason behind the theft, a misunderstanding that could be resolved with a conversation.

With a sigh, Sarah made her decision. "Alright, we'll confront the culprit. But first, let's see if there's any clue inside the bag that might point us in the right direction."

Unwrapping the sandwich carefully, Sarah examined its contents. Nestled amongst the lettuce and tomato slices was a small, folded piece of paper. Curiosity piqued, she unfolded it, her eyes widening as she recognized the loopy handwriting. It was a note, and it was addressed to her.

Part 4: A Change of Heart

The note clutched in Sarah's hand was a surprise twist in their lunchtime investigation. Unfolding the flimsy piece of paper, a single line scrawled in messy handwriting stared back at them: "Just borrowing a bite. Hangry monster at your service. - J."

The implications hung heavy in the air. The culprit wasn't a disgruntled intern or a master thief with a specific sandwich craving. It was someone who knew Sarah, someone who felt comfortable enough to borrow a bite (without permission, of course).

"J?" Sarah repeated, her voice laced with confusion. "Who could that be?"

Tom and Nancy exchanged glances, equally bewildered. The note offered a clue, but it was an enigmatic one. J could stand for anyone from the chatty Janice in marketing to the perpetually grumpy night janitor, Joe. The suspect pool had widened considerably.

Suddenly, a light bulb flickered on over Nancy's head. "Wait a minute!" she exclaimed, her eyes gleaming with excitement. "There is a new intern named Jessica who started this week. Maybe she's our mystery J?"

Intrigued by this possibility, the detective trio decided to investigate further. Sarah, with a newfound mission in mind, devoured her sandwich (minus a mysterious bite, of course). The familiar flavors brought a sense of comfort after the rollercoaster of emotions.

Fueled by a sandwich and a renewed sense of purpose, they made their way to Jessica's cubicle. The young intern, barely out of college, looked up from her computer screen with a startled expression as they approached.

"Hi Jessica," Sarah greeted her, a friendly smile plastered on her face. "We're just following up on something. Did you happen to see a blue whale lunch bag around here earlier?"

Jessica's cheeks flushed a rosy pink. She stammered for a moment before blurting out, "Oh, uh, that? Yes, I, uh..."

Taking a deep breath, she composed herself and confessed. "Okay, fine. I admit it. I saw your lunch bag and... well, I was starving. I just took a tiny bite, I swear! I was going to put it back, but then you came looking for it, and I panicked."

Relief washed over Sarah. The culprit wasn't a hardened criminal mastermind; it was a hungry intern who succumbed to the irresistible aroma of tuna salad. The anger that had simmered within her dissipated, replaced by a grudging understanding.

"I can understand the temptation," Sarah admitted, a hint of amusement in her voice. "That is a pretty delicious sandwich."

A sheepish grin spread across Jessica's face. "I'm so sorry, Sarah. I'll replace your lunch, I promise. And maybe you could teach me how to make it sometime?"

The initial shock of the missing lunch had transformed into an unexpected bonding experience. Sarah, touched by Jessica's honesty and hunger pangs, readily agreed. Tom and Nancy, ever the supportive colleagues, chimed in with playful advice about surviving the first few weeks of office life (including the importance of packing a substantial lunch).

News of the lunchtime caper, complete with the mysterious note and the culprit reveal, spread like wildfire throughout Acme Enterprises.

Sarah's "borrowed bite" sandwich became an office legend, a testament to the power of a well-crafted lunch and the importance of understanding between colleagues. As for Jessica, she not only learned a valuable lesson about workplace etiquette but also gained a new friend and a newfound appreciation for the art of the tuna salad sandwich.

Chapter 3: A Delicious Resolution

Part 1: A Promise of Redemption

The following morning, Sarah arrived at the office with a lightness in her step. The lunchtime escapade, though initially stressful, had left a rather pleasant aftertaste. Jessica's apology and genuine remorse had disarmed her anger, replaced by a sense of camaraderie.

Reaching for the handle of the refrigerator, a flicker of apprehension crossed her mind. Would she find another empty space where her lunch bag once resided? But as she opened the door, her worries vanished. Nestled amongst the usual yogurt cups and Tupperware containers sat a vibrant blue whale lunch bag.

Intrigued, Sarah retrieved it. Unlike her usual meticulously crafted lunch bag complete with whale clip, this one was adorned with a single, perfect sunflower. A small note peeked out from beneath the flower. Unfolding it, Sarah read a message scrawled in the same loopy handwriting from the previous day's note:

"Consider this a peace offering. Your tuna creation is even more delicious than I imagined. - J (The reformed hangry monster)"

A smile bloomed on Sarah's face. Jessica's gesture, both the sunflower and the presumed replacement lunch, was a sweet token of apology. Hunger pangs gnawed at her stomach, reminding her it was time to break her fast.

Unclipping the unfamiliar lunch bag, Sarah peeked inside. Nestled amongst colorful napkin layers was a sight that made her eyes widen. It was a sandwich, but unlike any she'd ever seen before. Layers of fluffy focaccia bread cradled a vibrant salad of mixed greens, sun-dried tomatoes, and avocado slices. But the real star of the show was a perfectly seared salmon fillet, its glistening skin hinting at its deliciousness.

On a small note tucked beside the sandwich was a single word: "Inspired."

Part 2: A Culinary Adventure

Sarah stared at the salmon salad sandwich, mesmerized. It was a culinary masterpiece, a symphony of textures and flavors that promised an explosion on the palate. But beyond the beauty of the sandwich itself, Sarah sensed a deeper message. This wasn't just lunch; it was a form of artistic expression, a response to Sarah's own creation.

A wave of respect washed over her. Jessica, it seemed, wasn't just hungry; she was also a fellow food enthusiast. Perhaps her desperate bite of Sarah's sandwich had awakened a dormant culinary passion within her.

Taking a seat at her desk, Sarah unwrapped the sandwich with reverence. The aroma of the perfectly seared salmon mingled with the tang of the sun-dried tomatoes and the sweetness of the avocado, creating a tantalizing fragrance that filled her senses. The first bite was a revelation. The salmon, cooked to a flaky perfection, burst with flavor in her mouth, complemented by the creamy avocado and the crisp lettuce. The tangy dressing tied everything together, creating a delectable harmony of textures and tastes.

As she savored each bite, Sarah felt a sense of satisfaction that transcended the mere act of eating. This wasn't just lunch; it was a bridge built between two people, a connection forged over a shared love of good food. It was a small moment, a quiet exchange of culinary creations within the sterile confines of an office break room, but it held the potential for something more – a budding friendship, perhaps even a lunchtime collaboration.

With a smile playing on her lips, Sarah finished the last bite of the exquisite salmon salad sandwich. Picking up a pen and a scrap of paper, she scribbled a quick note: "Thank you, J! Your culinary skills are truly inspiring. Now, how about a tuna salad-salmon hybrid creation for tomorrow's lunch?"

Folding the note, Sarah placed it on top of the empty salmon lunch bag. A sense of anticipation filled her. The "borrowed bite" incident had turned into something unexpected, a delicious adventure that had led to a newfound appreciation for a colleague and the power of a shared lunch. As she hit send on an email inviting Jessica to join her for coffee, Sarah couldn't help but wonder what culinary delights the future held. Perhaps Acme Enterprises' break room, once a stage for the mundane, was about to become a haven for gastronomic exploration, a place where lunchtime turned into a celebration of flavor, friendship, and, of course, the occasional borrowed bite.

Part 3: A New Friendship

News of the "Great Tuna Caper" and its delicious resolution spread like wildfire through Acme Enterprises. The break room became a stage of enthusiastic lunchtime discussions, filled with speculation about the next culinary creation the unlikely duo of Sarah and Jessica would unveil.

Sarah, initially hesitant to embrace her newfound fame, found herself enjoying the innocent attention. Colleagues raved about the salmon salad sandwich, some even requesting a "Jessica special" for their lunch orders. Jessica, overwhelmed by the sudden spotlight, initially blushed and stammered excuses about just "winging it." Yet, a spark of pride ignited in her eyes, and a newfound confidence seemed to bloom within her.

One sunny afternoon, Sarah found Jessica hovering by the refrigerator, a hesitant smile on her face. In her hand, she held a lunch bag adorned with a bright yellow daisy.

"Hey Sarah," Jessica greeted, her voice barely above a whisper. "I, uh, wanted to try that tuna and salmon hybrid you mentioned. Here's my take on it."

Sarah, her heart swelling with warmth, took the daisy-adorned lunch bag. Inside, nestled amongst vibrant lettuce leaves, was a sandwich unlike any she had seen before. Flakes of tuna mingled with delicately smoked salmon, creating a mosaic of textures. Diced red onion added a sharp counterpoint to the creamy avocado spread, while a drizzle of balsamic glaze promised a sweet and tangy finish.

"Wow, Jessica," Sarah breathed, mesmerized by the culinary construction. "This looks... incredible!"

Jessica puffed out her chest, a shy smile gracing her lips. "Just a little something I came up with."

Sarah, eager to taste this creative fusion, took a bite. The symphony of flavors exploded on her tongue – the richness of the salmon perfectly balanced by the familiar comfort of the tuna salad. The onion added a delightful bite, while the balsamic glaze tied everything together. It was a testament to Jessica's newfound culinary confidence, a creation that paid homage to Sarah's original masterpiece while adding a unique twist of her own.

As they sat together, devouring their respective lunch creations and exchanging culinary ideas, a sense of camaraderie filled the break room.

Other colleagues, drawn in by the aroma and the excited chatter, joined them, eager to hear about the latest lunchtime adventure.

The once-mundane break room had transformed into a hub of creativity and connection. Lunch wasn't just about sustenance anymore; it was about exploration, sharing, and forging friendships over a shared love of good food. And it all began with a single borrowed bite, a stolen sandwich, and a chance encounter between two unlikely culinary partners.

Part 4: A Culinary Legacy

The "Great Tuna Caper" became a legend at Acme Enterprises, whispered about in hushed tones and recounted with embellished details during watercooler conversations. Sarah and Jessica, the unlikely heroes of the lunchtime escapade, found themselves thrust into an unexpected spotlight.

While Sarah initially felt a touch overwhelmed by the sudden attention, she couldn't deny the joy it brought. Colleagues who were once distant acquaintances now approached her with eager questions about upcoming "lunchtime specials."

Jessica, on the other hand, blossomed under the newfound appreciation. Her shyness gradually melted away, replaced by a newfound confidence that shone in her bright eyes and the creative flourishes she added to their lunch creations.

The break room, once a place of quiet solitude and hastily consumed meals, transformed into a vibrant hub of lunchtime activity. Every day became an unveiling, a stage for Sarah and Jessica's culinary experiments. Office productivity seemed to increase, fueled by the anticipation of what delectable dish would grace the table next.

One sunny Tuesday, a particularly long and monotonous day stretched before them. As the clock struck noon, Sarah and Jessica arrived at the break room, their faces mirroring the general air of fatigue. But that changed the moment they unveiled their lunch bags.

Sarah's offering was a vibrant summer salad, a light and refreshing counterpoint to the heaviness of the day. A bed of mixed greens held a colorful bounty of sliced strawberries, crumbled feta cheese, and candied pecans. The star of the show, however, was a perfectly grilled chicken breast, seasoned with a unique blend of herbs that filled the room with an enticing aroma.

Jessica, not to be outdone, presented a culinary masterpiece that defied categorization. It was a deconstructed pizza, a playful twist on the classic lunchtime staple. A bed of crispy flatbread served as the base, topped with a vibrant tomato sauce and a generous scattering of melted mozzarella cheese. But instead of the usual pepperoni or sausage, Jessica had added a delightful surprise – pan-seared shrimp, their glistening shells hinting at their deliciousness. The dish was finished with a drizzle of pesto and a scattering of fresh basil leaves, an explosion of flavors that promised to tantalize the taste buds.

As their colleagues gathered around, drawn in by the mouthwatering aromas and the promise of a culinary adventure, Sarah and Jessica exchanged a knowing smile. The "Great Tuna Caper" might have been the spark that ignited their lunchtime partnership, but it was their shared passion and creativity that kept it burning. They had transformed the once-mundane into something extraordinary, a testament to the joy of collaboration and the power of a good lunch.

And so, the lunchtime saga continued at Acme Enterprises. With each passing day, Sarah and Jessica pushed the boundaries of their culinary creativity, their lunchtime creations becoming a source of inspiration and delight for their colleagues. They proved that even amidst the monotony of office life, a little spark of passion and a shared love of food could create a community, a friendship, and a whole lot of delicious memories. The story of the "Great Tuna Caper" served as a reminder – sometimes, the most unexpected things, like a stolen sandwich and a borrowed bite, can lead to the most delightful outcomes.

Chapter 4: A Culinary Challenge

Part 1: A Culinary Icon

The crisp autumn air swirled around Acme Enterprises, carrying with it the promise of changing seasons and a renewed sense of excitement. The summer's lunchtime salad creations had given way to heartier fare, with pumpkin spice and warm aromas filling the break room as Sarah and Jessica prepped for their latest culinary challenge.

It wasn't just another Tuesday lunch. Today marked the first official "Acme Eats" competition, a brainchild of Brenda, the ever-enthusiastic office manager, who saw the Sarah and Jessica phenomenon as a way to boost employee morale and camaraderie. The competition was simple: each department could nominate a team of two for a lunchtime cook-off, with Sarah and Jessica acting as judges alongside Brenda.

The air crackled with nervous anticipation as teams from Marketing, Sales, and IT set up their makeshift kitchens on designated tables in the break room. Sarah and Jessica, adorned with official-looking judge badges (courtesy of Brenda's boundless office supply collection), surveyed the scene with a mixture of excitement and apprehension.

The first team to present their creation was a duo from Marketing, known for their flamboyant personalities. They unveiled a towering "Meatloaf Mountain," a behemoth of a meatloaf slathered in a thick, ketchup-glazed sauce and surrounded by a moat of mashed potatoes. While impressive in size, Sarah and Jessica couldn't help but raise an eyebrow at the unabashedly 1950s diner vibe.

Next came the team from Sales, known for their fast-talking, competitive spirit. Their offering was a deconstructed sushi platter, an array of colorful ingredients artfully arranged on individual plates.

The sashimi slices were fresh, the seaweed salad crisp, but the overall presentation felt a tad sterile and lacked the warmth of a home-cooked meal.

Finally, it was IT's turn. Their team, two quiet programmers who typically kept to themselves, surprised everyone. They presented a steaming pot of fragrant Thai curry, accompanied by perfectly cooked jasmine rice and a colorful array of fresh vegetables. The aroma was heavenly, promising a burst of flavor that went beyond the usual lunchtime fare.

As Sarah, Jessica, and Brenda meticulously sampled each dish, a lively discussion ensued. The Marketing team's "Meatloaf Mountain" was praised for its sheer size but criticized for its lack of subtlety. The Sales team's deconstructed sushi was applauded for its freshness but deemed slightly uninspired. The IT team's Thai curry, on the other hand, garnered rave reviews. The complex flavors, vibrant colors, and perfect balance of textures had the judges leaning towards them as the frontrunners.

Part 2: A Company Tradition

The tension in the break room was thick enough to slice as the judges deliberated. Sarah, ever the champion of creativity and flavor, was particularly impressed by the IT team's Thai curry. Jessica, however, couldn't ignore the playful presentation and sheer audacity of the Marketing team's "Meatloaf Mountain." Brenda, the voice of reason amidst the culinary debate, argued for balance – a dish that was impressive without being overwhelming, delicious without being overly complex.

After much discussion and a few playful jabs at the "Meatloaf Mountain's" questionable aesthetics, the judges reached a decision. Brenda cleared her throat, a mischievous glint in her eyes.

"Alright everyone," she announced, her voice ringing out through the break room. "The votes are in, and the winner of the first Acme Eats competition is..."

A collective gasp filled the room as Brenda paused for dramatic effect.

"The IT department!" she declared, a wide smile spreading across her face.

The two IT programmers, usually reserved and quiet, beamed with pride. They had emerged from their cubicle shadows to become the unlikely champions of the first Acme Eats competition. As congratulations rained down upon them,

Sarah and Jessica presented them with a small trophy Brenda had conjured – a plastic spork glued to a coffee mug, emblazoned with the words "Acme Eats Champion." It might not have been gold, but it held a certain charm, a testament to their unexpected culinary triumph.

The success of the first Acme Eats competition sparked a wave of enthusiasm throughout Acme Enterprises. Departments started planning for future competitions, brainstorming themes and perfecting recipes. The break room, once a place of silence and solo lunches, became a bustling hub of culinary creativity. Colleagues who had previously never interacted found themselves sharing recipes and swapping cooking tips.

The spirit of friendly competition fostered a sense of camaraderie that transcended the walls of individual cubicles. The lunchtime routine, once a monotonous affair, became an exciting adventure, a chance to connect with colleagues and celebrate the joy of good food. Sarah and Jessica, the accidental catalysts of this culinary revolution, watched with a sense of satisfaction as their shared love of food brought people together.

But little did they know, a new challenge was brewing on the horizon, a challenge that would test their culinary skills and their newfound friendship in ways they never imagined. A challenge that would involve a surprise guest judge, a secret ingredient, and a recipe for disaster (or perhaps, an unexpected culinary masterpiece).

Part 3: A Symbol of Unity

The announcement for the next Acme Eats competition dropped like a culinary bomb. Not only would the theme be a mystery, but a surprise guest judge would be gracing them with their presence. The break room buzzed with speculation. Would it be a Michelin-starred chef? A celebrity food critic? The suspense was enough to turn the usually stale office air into a simmering pot of anticipation.

Brenda, the mastermind behind the competition's evolution, kept the details tightly under wraps. All participants knew was that the theme would be revealed on the day of the competition and the surprise judge would be a "renowned figure in the culinary world."

Sarah and Jessica, now seasoned competition veterans, found themselves at the center of the storm. Colleagues flocked to them, seeking advice on recipe ideas and menu planning.

Sarah, ever the practical one, focused on versatility and adaptable dishes that could be tweaked based on the mystery theme. Jessica, on the other hand, embraced the unknown, her mind swirling with wild and creative possibilities.

The day of the competition arrived, and the tension in the break room was electric. Each team, adorned with themed attire (Marketing – aprons printed with hot dogs, Sales – chef hats with dollar signs, IT – binary code printed tee-shirts), stood at their makeshift kitchens, a nervous energy crackling between them.

Finally, Brenda stepped onto a makeshift platform (a chair precariously balanced on a stack of office supplies). In her hand, she held a sealed envelope.

"Alright, everyone!" she boomed, her voice filled with excitement. "The time has come to unveil the theme of today's competition... and our esteemed guest judge!"

With a dramatic flourish, Brenda ripped open the envelope. A hush fell over the room as she scanned the contents. A wide grin spread across her face as she announced, "The theme for today's culinary challenge is... Leftovers!"

A collective groan rippled through the break room. Leftovers? Who could possibly create a masterpiece from yesterday's dinner scraps? But as the initial disappointment subsided, a spark of determination ignited in the eyes of the participants. After all, a good cook could turn even the most mundane ingredients into something extraordinary.

The final twist came with the unveiling of the guest judge. Brenda pulled back a curtain, revealing a figure standing regally behind it – Mildred Henderson, the notoriously grumpy head of accounting. Gasps of surprise filled the room. Mildred? The woman who practically scowled at the sight of a birthday cupcake?

As Mildred stepped into the spotlight, a mischievous twinkle shone in her usually stern eyes. "Alright, everyone," she declared in a surprisingly cheerful voice, "Let's see who can transform yesterday's dinner into today's gourmet delight!"

The competition was on. Sarah and Jessica, initially surprised by the unconventional theme and judge, found themselves invigorated. They had always championed the art of repurposing leftovers, and here was their chance to showcase their skills. With a renewed sense of purpose, they joined the other teams, the break room once again transformed into a bustling culinary arena.

But while the competition spirit raged on, a small, forgotten detail remained – the mystery within the mystery. What secret ingredient would Brenda unveil, an ingredient that could elevate a dish or send it crashing down in flames?

Part 4: A Culinary Legacy

The revelation of leftovers as the competition theme had initially dampened the mood, but it quickly ignited a spark of creative defiance. Participants scurried back to their stations, rummaging through their lunch bags and pulling out the remnants of yesterday's meals – a lonely chicken breast, a forgotten container of mac and cheese, a half-eaten bag of steamed vegetables.

Sarah and Jessica, ever the resourceful duo, surveyed their own meager offerings: a leftover salmon fillet and a side of steamed asparagus.

While it wasn't much, their minds buzzed with possibilities. They could create a delicate salmon en papillote, a dish steamed in parchment paper that promised to retain the fish's moisture and flavor. The asparagus, with a touch of creativity, could be transformed into a vibrant side salad.

Just as they were finalizing their plan, Brenda entered the room, a mischievous glint in her eyes. In her hand, she held a small, wicker basket overflowing with... mystery ingredients.

"Now, now," she announced, her voice dripping with mock seriousness, "before you get too comfortable with your leftover comfort food, let me introduce the wildcard element!"

A collective gasp filled the room as Brenda revealed the basket's contents: a selection of exotic fruits – dragon fruit with its vibrant pink flesh, starfruit with its star-shaped cross-section, and passion fruit bursting with a tangy aroma.

The challenge had just gotten a whole lot more interesting. Now, the participants had to not only elevate their leftover dishes but also incorporate these unusual fruits into their creations. Some groaned, overwhelmed by the unexpected twist. Others, eyes gleaming with excitement, saw it as an opportunity to truly wow the judges – especially the surprisingly enthusiastic Mildred.

Sarah and Jessica exchanged a glance, a silent conversation passing between them. This was a challenge they could relish. The dragon fruit's vibrant pink hue could add a stunning visual element to their salmon dish, while the passion fruit's tangy sweetness could create a delightful sauce. The starfruit, with its unique shape, could be used as a decorative garnish, adding a touch of whimsy to their creation.

The break room buzzed with renewed activity. The air, once filled with the aroma of reheated leftovers, now held a hint of exotic sweetness. Teams huddled together, chopping, mixing, and brainstorming, the sound of sizzling pans and whispered strategies filling the air.

With time ticking away, the pressure mounted. Sarah and Jessica worked in a synchronized flow, their movements fueled by creative energy. The salmon, seasoned with a touch of citrus, was carefully wrapped in parchment paper with the sliced dragon fruit. The asparagus, tossed with a light vinaigrette, awaited its final flourish.

Finally, the buzzer sounded, signaling the end of the competition. A wave of exhaustion and nervous anticipation swept through the room. Each team, with trembling hands, presented their dishes to the judges.

Brenda, surprisingly enthusiastic, sampled each creation with gusto. Mildred, perched on her makeshift throne of office supplies, maintained a stern expression, but a hint of curiosity flickered in her eyes as she meticulously examined each dish.

One by one, the teams presented their revamped leftovers. Sales had transformed their leftover steak into a fajita fiesta, complete with a vibrant salsa incorporating the starfruit. Marketing had deconstructed their chili into a chili cheese dip, adorned with dragon fruit pearls. The IT team, ever the underdogs, surprised everyone with a leftover pasta dish reborn as a creamy carbonara with a passion fruit twist.

Finally, it was Sarah and Jessica's turn. They presented their salmon en papillote, its parchment paper puffed up with steam. As Brenda carefully unfolded it, revealing the vibrant pink salmon nestled amidst the asparagus and dragon fruit slices, a collective gasp filled the room. Mildred, for the first time, cracked a genuine smile. The aroma that wafted from the dish was a symphony of sweet and savory, a testament to the unexpected flavors that had come together.

After a tense silence, Brenda and Mildred conferred, their whispers barely audible. Finally, Brenda cleared her throat and announced, "The winner of the second Acme Eats competition is..."

A drumroll of suspense filled the break room. Brenda paused for dramatic effect before declaring, "Sarah and Jessica!"

Cheers erupted through the room as Sarah and Jessica exchanged a high-five, a mixture of relief and exhilaration washing over them. They had not only overcome the challenge of leftovers but also incorporated the mystery ingredient in a way that surprised and delighted the judges.

As the excitement subsided, a newfound respect settled over the room. The competition had been more than just a culinary showdown; it was a testament to the ingenuity of ordinary people and the power of unexpected ingredients to transform the mundane into the extraordinary.

And as everyone gathered around the makeshift tables, enjoying the diverse creations born from leftovers and a touch of the exotic, they knew that the spirit of Acme Eats would continue

Chapter 5: The Sandwich's Legacy

Part 1: A Culinary Feud

The success of the Acme Eats competitions had transformed the once-sterile break room into a vibrant hub of culinary creativity. Every Tuesday lunchtime became an eagerly anticipated event, a stage for both seasoned cooks and enthusiastic novices to showcase their skills. Sarah and Jessica, the accidental champions who had sparked this culinary revolution, found themselves at the center of it all.

However, the newfound spirit of competition wasn't without its challenges. A simmering tension began to develop between the usually friendly Marketing and Sales teams. Their rivalry, fueled by years of vying for top sales figures, started to spill over into the culinary arena.

It all began with the "Ultimate Quesadilla Showdown." Marketing, known for their flashy presentations, created a quesadilla mountain, a towering structure filled with an assortment of cheeses and meats. Sales, ever the strategists, countered with a deconstructed "Quesadilla Symphony," a display of individual mini-quesadillas filled with gourmet ingredients.

While both creations were impressive in their own way, the judges (Sarah, Jessica, and a rotating cast of guest judges) felt they lacked the heart of a home-cooked meal. The focus, they remarked, seemed to be on outdoing each other rather than on creating a delicious and satisfying dish.

The judges' comments, intended to be constructive, struck a chord with some in Marketing and Sales. They took it as a personal attack, a challenge to their culinary prowess and, by extension, their salesmanship. The lighthearted competition began to morph into a bitter feud, with each team determined to prove their culinary dominance.

The tension reached a boiling point during the "Global Street Food Challenge." Marketing, in a flamboyant display, presented a "World on a Plate," a fusion dish that combined elements from various street food cultures. It was visually stunning, but the flavors clashed, leaving the judges confused and slightly nauseated.

Sales, determined to capitalize on Marketing's misstep, presented a seemingly simple dish – a classic Thai Pad See Ew. However, their attempt to elevate the dish with gourmet ingredients backfired. The expensive truffle oil overpowered the delicate balance of flavors, leaving the judges yearning for the familiar comfort of a well-made Pad See Ew.

The atmosphere in the break room was thick with disappointment and simmering anger. The joy of cooking and sharing had been replaced by a competitive anxiety. Sarah and Jessica, witnessing the downward spiral of what they had created, felt a sense of despair. The spirit of Acme Eats, once a celebration of food and camaraderie, was in danger of being extinguished.

Part 2: A Culinary Inspiration

The following Tuesday, a heavy silence hung over the break room. The once-bustling atmosphere of culinary excitement was replaced by a palpable sense of disappointment. The "Global Street Food Challenge" disaster had left a sour taste in everyone's mouth, figuratively and literally.

Sarah and Jessica, the heart and soul of Acme Eats, stood by the makeshift judges' table, their faces etched with concern. They exchanged a worried glance, both understanding the gravity of the situation. The playful competition they had nurtured was teetering on the brink of a full-blown office feud.

Determined to reignite the spirit of the competition, Sarah took a deep breath and addressed the room. "Everyone," she began, her voice resonating through the quiet space, "I know the past couple of weeks haven't been...ideal." A smattering of nods confirmed her observation.

"We all came here to celebrate food, to share our passion for cooking," Jessica chimed in, her voice brimming with a hopeful optimism. "But somewhere along the line, the focus shifted from enjoyment to competition."

A few brave souls offered mumbled agreements.

Sensing a receptive audience, Sarah continued, "There's nothing wrong with a little friendly competition, but let's not forget the true essence of Acme Eats. It's not about who has the most expensive ingredients or the flashiest presentation. It's about creating delicious dishes, sharing them with colleagues, and fostering a sense of community."

Her words seemed to resonate with the crowd. Heads nodded in agreement, and a flicker of the old enthusiasm seemed to return to some eyes.

Taking advantage of the receptive mood, Sarah announced a change in plans. "Instead of individual team challenges," she declared, "how about we collaborate this time? Let's create a global potluck feast, each team bringing a dish from a different region."

A murmur of surprised approval rippled through the room. The idea of working together, of celebrating the diversity of global cuisine, seemed to appeal to the competitive spirit in a more positive way.

"We can draw regions from a hat," Jessica suggested, a playful smile lighting up her face.

"That way, it's a surprise for everyone, and each team has to step outside their comfort zone."

The suggestion met with enthusiastic cheers. The spirit of competition was still alive, but this time it was channeled into a collaborative effort, a celebration of culinary diversity rather than a battle for dominance.

As the excitement grew, Sarah and Jessica surveyed the room, a sense of relief washing over them. The culinary feud may have threatened the spirit of Acme Eats, but a simple shift in focus, a reminder of the core values, had rekindled the flame. The break room was poised to once again be a haven for creativity, a place where food became a bridge between colleagues, fostering connections and creating a sense of community, one delicious bite at a time.

Part 3: A Symbol of Hope

The "Global Potluck Feast" turned out to be a resounding success. The competitive spirit simmered beneath the surface, but this time it fueled a collaborative energy. Teams huddled together, researching recipes, planning menus, and sourcing ingredients. Laughter and enthusiastic discussions filled the air, replacing the previous tension with a sense of camaraderie.

The day of the potluck arrived, and the break room transformed into a vibrant celebration of global flavors. Marketing, tasked with Latin America, brought a vibrant platter of sizzling fajitas, their colorful presentation redeemed by the delicious and authentic flavors. Sales, responsible for Southeast Asia, surprised everyone with a fragrant Thai Green Curry, the perfect balance of spice and creaminess impressing even the most discerning palate.

The IT team, assigned to Europe, presented a classic French Quiche Lorraine, its golden brown crust and creamy filling a testament to their newfound culinary confidence. Even Brenda, the ever-enthusiastic office manager, joined in the fun, showcasing her family's secret recipe for Italian meatballs, their richness and tenderness drawing appreciative groans from the crowd.

As colleagues mingled, sampling each other's offerings and exchanging cooking tips, the spirit of Acme Eats truly came alive.

The competition had faded into the background, replaced by a shared appreciation for food and the joy of creating something delicious together.

Sarah and Jessica, watching from the corner of the room, felt a surge of satisfaction. Their intervention had salvaged the spirit of Acme Eats, channeling the competitive energy into a collaborative experience. The potluck feast was more than just a meal; it was a celebration of teamwork, a reminder that even in the cutthroat world of office politics, a shared love of food could bridge divides and foster a sense of belonging.

The success of the potluck feast marked a turning point for Acme Eats. The competition continued, but in a more lighthearted and collaborative spirit. Teams focused on creating unique and delicious dishes, always open to feedback and learning from each other. Sarah and Jessica continued to act as mentors and guides, encouraging experimentation and fostering a supportive environment.

Acme Eats became a cornerstone of office life, a weekly ritual that not only fostered camaraderie but also boosted morale and productivity. The break room, once a sterile and uninspiring space, transformed into a vibrant hub of culinary creativity. The aroma of exotic spices mingled with the comforting scent of home-cooked meals, creating a sensory experience that transcended the boundaries of the office walls.

And so, the story of Acme Eats continued, a testament to the power of food to bring people together, to spark creativity, and to remind everyone that even the most mundane lunch break can be an opportunity for connection, collaboration, and a whole lot of delicious fun.

Part 4: A Culinary Legacy

News of Acme Eats and its transformative power spread beyond the walls of the office. Local news outlets picked up the story, intrigued by the company's unique approach to employee engagement. Soon, Acme Enterprises found itself at the center of a mini-culinary phenomenon. Other companies, seeking to replicate the positive impact of Acme Eats, reached out to Sarah and Jessica for advice.

One sunny afternoon, a delegation from a neighboring tech company, known for its high-pressure environment and low employee morale, arrived at Acme Enterprises. Sarah and Jessica, initially nervous about sharing their "secret sauce," found themselves surprised by the genuine interest and enthusiasm in the visitors' eyes.

Over a lunch of leftover Thai Green Curry and Brenda's famous meatballs (a staple in the break room ever since the potluck feast), Sarah and Jessica shared their journey. They spoke about the unexpected birth of Acme Eats, the challenges of the competitive feud, and the ultimate triumph of collaboration.

The visitors hung onto their every word, their eyes filled with hope and a touch of envy. As Sarah finished recounting the story of the Global Potluck Feast, a woman from the delegation spoke up.

"It sounds incredible," she admitted. "But how do we get started? How do we create a similar sense of community in our own company?"

Jessica, ever the optimist, leaned forward. "It all starts with a shared love of food," she declared. "Begin with a simple potluck, encourage colleagues to bring dishes from their heritage or favorite cuisine. Let them share their stories, their recipes. Food has a way of breaking down barriers and fostering connections."

Sarah chimed in, adding a touch of caution. "Don't force competition at first. Let the focus be on sharing and enjoying different flavors and traditions. If a friendly competition arises organically later, it can be a positive force. But always remember, the core value is about creating a sense of community, not about culinary dominance."

The delegation left Acme Enterprises that afternoon inspired and armed with a roadmap for creating their own version of Acme Eats. As Sarah and Jessica watched them depart, they realized the impact of their lunch break revolution had extended beyond the walls of their own company.

Acme Eats had become a beacon of hope, a testament to the power of food to bridge divides and foster a sense of belonging. It was a reminder that even in the sterile environment of an office, a little creativity and a shared passion for something as simple (and delicious) as food could create a community, spark joy, and transform the ordinary into something truly extraordinary.

And so, the story of Acme Eats continued to unfold, a testament to the enduring power of food, community, and the unexpected culinary adventures that unfolded one delicious lunch break at a time.

About the Author

Mrigendra Bharti, born on June 29, 2004, in South Delhi, India, is a multifaceted individual recognized as the owner of Mrigendra Bharti Group InfoTech India Co. Pvt Ltd. Beyond his entrepreneurial endeavors, he is a distinguished music producer, director, and a budding writer.

Embarking on his professional journey at a young age, Mrigendra Bharti's visionary leadership has led to the establishment of several successful ventures, including Croma Music Series Entertainment, Sellbrochure, Fauget Innovative, and more.

What sets Mrigendra apart is his early initiation into the world of business. His foray into the unknown realms of entrepreneurship began during his 10th-grade years, where he delved into the music industry. This initial venture laid the foundation for subsequent achievements, showcasing his dedication and resilience.

Having honed his skills in music, Mrigendra Bharti not only demonstrated significant growth in his craft but also expanded his professional network. His passion extends beyond music, encompassing app and website development, as well as graphic design.

Fueled by his creative aspirations, Mrigendra established the Mrigendra Bharti Group, a company specializing in website and app development. Currently, he collaborates with a dedicated team, collectively working on ambitious projects that promise innovation and excellence.

Mrigendra's journey serves as an inspiration, particularly for today's students, highlighting the potential of youthful determination and the ability to transform innovative ideas into successful businesses. As he continues to make strides in various domains, Mrigendra Bharti remains a dynamic force, contributing vibrancy to the realms of business, music, and technology.

Read more at https://www.imwriter-mrigendra.rf.gd.